Condemned by Fate

A Short Story Prequel to

The Ambition & Destiny Series

By
VL McBeath

Condemned by Fate
By V L McBeath

Editing services provided by **The Pro Book Editor**

Cover design by Michelle Abrahall

ISBN: 978-0-9955708-0-1 (Kindle Edition)
978-0-9955708-3-2 (Paperback)

Main category—Fiction / Short Stories (Single Author)
Other category— Fiction / Romance / Historical / Victorian

First Edition

Legal Notices

Explanatory Notes

Meal times

In the United Kingdom, as in many parts of the world, meal times are referred to by a variety of names. Based on traditional working class practices in northern England in the 19th Century, the following terms have been used in this book:

Breakfast: The meal eaten upon rising each morning.

Dinner: The meal eaten around midday. This may be a hot or cold meal depending on the day of the week and a person's occupation.

Tea: Not to be confused with the high tea of the aristocracy or the beverage of the same name, tea was the meal eaten at the end of the working day, typically around five or six o'clock. This could either be a hot or cold meal.

Money

In 1839, the currency in the United Kingdom was Pounds, Shillings and Pence.

- There were twenty shillings to each pound and twelve pence to a shilling.
- The value of £1 in 1839 is equivalent to approximately £100 in 2018

  (Ref: http://www.bankofengland.co.uk/monetary-policy/inflation)

For further information on Victorian England visit:
https://valmcbeath.com/victorian-era-england-1837-1901/

Please note: This book is written in UK English

Some words use the old English spelling

Aldridge, near Birmingham, England. August 1843

CHARLES FEARED THAT THE NEXT time he fell asleep would be the last. His body ached and an overwhelming fatigue had settled on him. Until a few days ago, he thought he was getting better. Then the fever started, and now he wasn't so sure.

He wasn't afraid of dying but wished the prospect hadn't come upon him so quickly. He was only twenty-three years old. There was still so much to look forward to, so many things he wanted to do, but he suspected they were beyond him now. As he fought the urge to close his eyes, he looked around the room he'd been confined to for the last month. Not that there was much to see. Other than the double bed he occupied there was only a dresser with a jug and wash bowl sat on top, and a wooden dining chair to his left. Nothing hung from the whitewashed walls. Unusually, the chair was empty. He'd been asleep, so the family must have thought they could slip away. He prayed the next person he saw would be Mary.

The coughing started again without warning and he thought it would split his chest in two. It sapped what little energy he had left, but had the effect of bringing his sister into the room. Louisa was four years older than him, and alongside Mary had been his principal nurse over these last few weeks.

"That's it, cough it all out," Louisa said as she arranged his pillows. "We need to get you breathing again. I've opened your window and the front door to get a draught through; that should help."

"M-Mary…" Charles said.

"She'll be here soon. She's outside with William at the moment. Lie still and rest. I'll sit with you until she arrives."

Charles shivered as a warm breeze crossed over him, but didn't have the energy to pull the blanket higher. Instead, he closed his eyes and tried to focus on breathing. His chest rattled as it rose and fell, and the unhurried rhythm dulled his consciousness. Gradually Mary's face filled his mind. She was smiling at him, her beautiful blue eyes dancing with delight as she reached out to draw him to her. With the sun glistening on her light brown hair, she had never looked more beautiful. How could he resist? He drifted towards her, took her in his arms and kissed her as if his life depended on it.

A smile flickered across his face as he remembered the first day they met. His life changed forever that summer of 1839.

It was the end of June when he went to her father's farm to help protect the crops from the excessive rain. Mary was collecting eggs when he arrived, and he approached her to ask after her father. At first he thought she was little more than a child, but when she stood up, he realised her dark grey pinafore dress concealed the figure of a young woman, and a fine one at that.

"I'm looking for Mr Chadwick," Charles said not taking his eyes off her.

"He's up in the top field." She nodded beyond the house. "He'll be down for dinner soon enough. You'd be as well waiting here."

"I've got my things." He raised a linen bag and pointed at it. "Can I take them inside?"

"Mother's in the kitchen …"

"Perhaps I'll wait and let you introduce me."

Mary's cheeks flushed red and Charles smiled when she turned away to compose herself.

"I'm not sure I can introduce someone I don't know," she said as she surveyed the fields.

"I'm Charles," he said, broadening his smile. "I'm here to help your father with the drainage."

*

Mr Chadwick was an acquaintance of his father and Charles didn't know him well. He'd met him a couple of times, but following a chance meeting the previous week in Aldridge, he'd offered him the job in exchange for a few shillings a week and free board and lodgings. Having nothing better to do, Charles thought he might as well take him up on the offer. Following dinner, the two of them walked through the fields together. When they got to the farthest field, Charles saw several other labourers already digging.

"I won't be on my own, then," Charles said.

"There's too much to do for one," Mr Chadwick said. "We need to get these trenches dug as soon as possible. We've got potatoes, turnips and carrots almost ready for harvesting, but another day of rain could ruin me."

"Hey, Charlie." It was Mr Chadwick's son, John. "Pa told me you were joining us, what's up? Is there no work in Aldridge?" Charles hadn't seen John since last summer, but with his head of ginger hair, he wasn't easy to forget.

"I fancied a change and it's better than working for my old man. At least here I'll get a bit of beer money."

John laughed. "I guess we'll be seeing you at the tavern tonight, then. It's dominos night."

"That's enough," Mr Chadwick said. "You won't be earning anything if you don't start digging."

Fortunately, the rain stayed away and the men made good progress with the trenches. When the sun was still an hour from the horizon, Charles returned to the yard with John and Mr Chadwick. They washed their hands in a large barrel of water standing at the corner of the house before they went into the kitchen. It looked as if they were expected. The table standing in the middle of the room was laden with bread, butter, cheese and ale. The pan sitting over the fire released a smell that made his mouth water.

"Just find a chair and sit yourself down," Mrs Chadwick said. "No standing on ceremony here. Have you met the girls? This is Susannah, Alice, Mary and Katharine."

"I've met Mary." He took the opportunity to rest his eyes on her again. This time she returned his gaze and the clear blue of her eyes held him captivated.

"Mary and I are twins," Alice said, breaking the moment.

"So you are." Charles looked at Alice and then back to Mary. "Not quite identical, though."

"All right, that's enough," Mrs Chadwick said. "Get yourselves sat down and let Pa say grace."

Once he finished, Mrs Chadwick served out steaming bowls of soup and offered around the bread. Everyone ate in silence, giving Charles the opportunity to steal an occasional glance at Mary. At first he thought she was ignoring him, but as the meal went on, he was delighted to find she was gazing at him when she thought he wasn't looking. The first time their eyes met, her cheeks coloured and she turned away.

Condemned by Fate

That evening he went to the tavern with John. They were late back and, except for a single candle flickering on the kitchen table, the house was in darkness. Once he got into bed, he couldn't get Mary from his mind. It was a strange feeling. He'd met plenty of other girls, but none had ever made him feel the way she did.

The following morning Mary was in the kitchen when he came down for breakfast. She looked charming in her clean pinafore dress with her hair swept into a bun at the nape of her neck. She smiled as he walked in and offered him a bowl of porridge, which he accepted. He was about to leave the table when she put down a plate of scrambled eggs.

"Is that for me?" Charles asked.

"I expect you'll need it. Pa says it's hard work in the fields all day."

He wasn't used to eating so much but wasn't going to turn it down, especially not when she sat opposite and watched him eat every mouthful.

"Would you like some more?" she said once he had finished.

His stomach was uncomfortable, but how could he say no when she looked at him like that?

"I wish I could but …"

"What are you still doing here?" Mr Chadwick said as he walked into the kitchen. "You should be gone by now."

"I'm going. I just need to put my boots on."

"Well see that's all you do," Mr Chadwick picked up his cap. "I'll catch you up later. I need to speak to Mrs Chadwick first."

"I've put some food in a box for your dinner," Mary said once her father had gone. "It's only some bread and cheese, but it'll keep you going until you get back tonight."

"Won't you bring it to the field for me? It'd be a blessing to see someone as lovely as you, even if it is only for a few minutes."

"My place is here." Mary's cheeks coloured once again. "I'll see you tonight."

Charles left the kitchen wondering what was happening to him. Only yesterday he had arrived in Shenstone with nothing more on his mind than earning a few shillings. Now he couldn't get Mary out of his mind. Was it her eyes? The way she looked at him was special, but there had to be more than that. Maybe it was her smile and the way she seemed to save it just for him.

He arrived in the field to find the locals there already.

"What time do you call this?" Thomas Baker said. "We've been here hours."

"Time you minded your own business," Charles said. "I'm a guest of the family. It'd be rude to leave without breakfast."

"All right for some. Your dad wouldn't be so lenient."

"Why d'you think I'm here?" Charles said with a laugh.

"Now you've finally arrived, you can come and help me with this trench. The soil's like clay and I'm done in."

Charles and Thomas worked all morning, but by the time Mr Chadwick joined them they had little to show for it.

"Is this as far as you've got?"

"The ground's solid." Charles banged his spade on the ground.

"The lads in the next field have done three times as much as you." Mr Chadwick nodded towards them.

"I bet the field down there isn't as waterlogged," Charles said. "Tell them we'll swap with them, see how they get on here."

"Less of your lip. I want this finished by the end of the day. Do you hear?"

As the day wore on, the clouds that had threatened rain in the morning started to clear and the sun beat down on them. Normally he would be pleased, but not today. He was exhausted and the sun didn't help.

There was no way they were going to finish that trench today, even if they stayed until sundown. When they saw the lads in the other field packing up, he suggested to Thomas that they do the same. He didn't need much persuading and they set off together across the field, picking their way through the rows of turnips. Part way down, Thomas jumped over a gate and headed towards Shenstone leaving Charles to walk back alone.

As he approached the farmyard, he saw Mary standing by the gate. She had a basket in her hands and looked as if she'd been collecting eggs, although why she would stop by the gate, he wasn't sure. He hoped she was waiting for him. She didn't see him straight away and he watched her petting one of the dogs. Maybe one day he could get her to fuss over him the way she did the animals.

With his aching muscles no longer at the front of his mind, he continued walking, trying unsuccessfully to wipe the mud from his shirt as he went.

"Are you done for the day?" she asked when she saw him.

"I am, and looking forward to lying on the grass once tea is over. We haven't had many sunny days this summer and I want to make the most of this. Your father's a hard task master."

"He's worried about the crops."

"I'm glad he is, otherwise I wouldn't be here. Not that I want them to come to any harm, you understand.

"No, of course." Mary looked down at the basket she was carrying. "I suppose I'd better get back with these."

"Don't go, not yet. I hardly know you. How old are you?"

"Nineteen. Why? What about you?"

"The same. I guessed you were younger than me."

"And I thought you were older." Mary gazed into his dark brown eyes. "You don't look like a minor."

Neither of them spoke for what felt like an eternity and Charles shifted from one foot to the other as he searched for something to say.

"I'd like to get to know you better," he said. "Join me on the grass later; I'll sit on that little bit in the middle of the yard so no one need worry about you."

"I can't," Mary said as they walked back to the house. "I've some darning to do and Mother likes us all to sit with her."

"Would she miss you for five minutes?" Charles said. "Tell her you dropped your handkerchief and need to find it."

"If I tell her that and then she sees me on the grass with you, she'll know I'm lying."

A smile spread across Charles's face. "Maybe I can miss a few minutes rest and help you look for it."

"We could sit around the corner, away from the window." Mary nodded towards the piece of grass by the side of the house. "Then she won't notice."

They reached the back door before Charles could answer, but he wasn't going to argue. It was just a shame they needed to eat.

The rest of the family were seated and Charles took his place at the table next to John. The room fell silent as Mr Chadwick stood up to say grace before his wife served out a vegetable stew with dumplings. Charles didn't want to be in the kitchen for any longer than necessary and was grateful for the lack of conversation as he wolfed down his food. While everyone ate, he glanced at Mary in the hope that she was as eager as he was to be outside again. The smile fell from his face when he noticed she hadn't touched her food. Had she changed her mind?

He waited for Mr Chadwick to clear his plate before he asked to be excused from the table. With permission granted, he made his way to the kitchen door only to hear Mrs Chadwick ask Mary to help collect up the dirty dishes.

"I'm sorry, would you mind if Alice does it," Mary said. "I need to go outside. I've gone very hot in here; I need some air."

"Why do I have to do it?" Alice asked.

"And what about the darning?" her mother said.

"I can do the darning when I come back. Please. I'm sure I'll feel better after a walk."

Charles didn't wait to hear the end of the conversation but went to the side of the house in the hope that Mary would follow him. He had barely settled on the grass when she rounded the corner with a smile on her face.

"I thought you weren't feeling well?" he said.

"Was I convincing?"

"You were so good I thought you were ill."

"I'm always good."

"Maybe it's time we changed that?" Charles grinned at her.

"I don't know what you mean." She tucked her long skirt into her legs and rested one hand on the ground as she sat down.

"Why didn't you eat your food tonight?"

"I wasn't hungry," she said, studying some clover near her hand.

"Perhaps you are ill, then. You should be hungry when you haven't eaten all day."

Mary flushed and turned her attention to the horizon. "I haven't got long. Mother will be expecting me back."

"Does she expect you to help her every evening?"

"If there's mending to do, we share it between us. She can't do it all on her own. I'd better go; there's a lot to do tonight."

"Another minute," Charles reached to tuck a stray piece of hair behind her ear. "I'm not going to hurt you. I think you're beautiful."

He let his hand rest on her shoulder, and when she smiled, he ran the back of his fingers down her cheek and onto her neck. Sensing no resistance, he moved down her arm and placed his hand on hers. It felt soft to his rough skin, and he lifted it to his lips and kissed each finger, never once taking his eyes off her. He had never felt this way about a woman before and a shiver ran through his body. His heart banged against his chest as he leaned forward and her lips, full and red, parted in anticipation. He could think of nothing but taking her in his arms and making her his own. As their lips touched, every fibre of his being felt alive, but suddenly and without explanation, he stopped. He released her hand and fixed his attention on a butterfly that floated above the flowers in the wall. He shouldn't be doing this, not to someone so special. It would ruin her. As the butterfly moved away, he became aware of

Mary fidgeting beside him. Knowing he couldn't trust himself, he stood up and pretended to look out over the fields.

"I'm going for a walk," he said. "Will you come with me?"

"A walk? I thought … No, I'm sorry, I have to get back."

"Yes, of course, the darning. Perhaps tomorrow?"

"Perhaps," she said, her smile fading. "If Mother doesn't need me."

Charles watched her walk away, her back erect and regal before he spun around and kicked the wall. What was he thinking? She was the most wonderful girl he had ever met and he had stood up to go for a walk. What an idiot. He needed to speak to her tomorrow and hope she accepted his apology.

*

The rain started around mid-morning the following day and grew heavier as time went on. The ground, which was sodden, turned into mud pits and by the time Charles came back to the house, he was wet and filthy. John and Mr Chadwick had walked ahead of him and, thinking he was alone, he went to the water butt at the side of the barn and plunged his hands in before throwing water over his face and head. With water dripping down his face and back, he looked for Mary, but his shoulders slumped when he failed to see her. He shook his head to remove the water from his hair and as he did, he noticed a movement from the corner of his eye. She was there, standing in the doorway of the barn.

"What are you doing out?" he said. "You'll catch your death out here."

"I-I'm sheltering from the rain. It's you we should be worried about. You're soaked to the skin."

"I'll dry soon enough." He ran his fingers through his tangled hair.

"It matches your eyes. Your hair, that is, dark and brown."

"I suppose it does. I've never thought about it." He studied his feet as he kicked mud from his boots. "Listen, I'm sorry about last night. I didn't mean to walk away. I just needed some time."

"I shouldn't have been so forward."

"No, please, it wasn't your fault. I like you … a lot. Will you wait for me in the yard of an evening, then we can spend some time together without everyone else being around?"

"I don't know; I'd need a reason. I should be helping Mother at that time."

"I'm sure you can think of something, if you want to that is."

Mary glanced at the floor before she gazed back into his eyes.

"Oh yes, I want to."

*

As Charles walked down to the house the next afternoon, he was delighted to see Mary in the yard. She had been collecting eggs again, but her smile dropped when she saw he was not alone.

"What are you doing out?" John said to her.

"Collecting eggs. Mother didn't manage to do it earlier."

"Can I take the basket for you?" Charles said.

"Thank you, but there's no need. I haven't finished yet."

"Well, don't be long. I'm starving." John spoke as he carried on walking.

"Let me help you," Charles took the basket and ushered Mary into the barn. "Will you be able to do this every day? I'll make sure I walk down from the fields alone if you can."

"I'll try. It's so difficult to be alone around here. It's a wonder Alice hasn't followed me. She's never far away."

"I know the feeling. Whenever I'm at home, there's always someone telling me what to do."

"Do you have brothers and sisters?"

Charles laughed. "Just a few. Seven sisters and my brother Richard. One sister's married and lives in Birmingham, but the rest are still at home."

"That's worse than here."

"It's not too bad, but I wish I could get away. Move to Birmingham, you know. Settle down."

"Mother says Birmingham's awful. Too many people."

Charles put the basket down and took hold of Mary's hands.

"It depends what you want, I suppose. If you're with the right person, it shouldn't matter." The blue of her eyes drew him to her and he leaned forward and kissed her gently on the lips. "It shouldn't matter at all."

They met most days after that, but as July turned into August, a leaden feeling settled in Charles's gut. He knew he needed to go home; the problem was that he didn't want to leave. He managed to stretch his work out for another week, but when he knew his time was up, he walked down to the yard earlier than usual and found Mary in the barn. Taking the basket from her, he sat her down on a low pile of hay, well hidden from view, and put his arms around her.

"You know I need to go home," he said, pulling her close. "I can't put it off any longer. I promised Father I'd be back by the end of July and we're now into August."

"You can't go," Mary turned to face him. "When will I see you again?"

"Soon, I promise. I'll be finished with the harvest by Michaelmas, and you can come to the harvest supper with me. It's only at the end of September."

"That's weeks away," she said, unable to stop her eyes filling with tears. "Please don't go. Father needs help with the harvest here."

"Don't cry," he said as the tears ran down her cheeks. "I'll be back, and I'll come over each Sunday as well if I can."

"I don't want to be here without you." She pressed her cheek against his chest. "I love you."

Charles leaned away and lifted her chin so their eyes met. As her tears continued to fall, he kissed them away, untroubled by their saltiness, before he moved to her lips and guided her onto the hay bales behind them. She didn't resist. With his heart racing, Charles continued to kiss her face and neck.

"I love you too," he said, freeing her hair from its ties. "I want to spend the rest of my life with you."

"Really?" Mary said, forcing Charles to stop and look at her.

"Really … will you marry me?"

Mary laughed through her tears. "Of course I will, but—"

A noise startled them. Charles turned around and jumped to his feet when he saw Mr Chadwick heading towards them.

"What the hell are you doing?" he yelled, lunging at Charles.

Charles froze and in an instant Mr Chadwick was upon him, his right fist slamming into his stomach. Charles doubled over and gasped, trying to get his breath back, but Mr Chadwick struck him again and again.

"What have you done to her? If you've dishonoured her, may God help me, I'll kill you."

"I haven't, I swear," Charles said. "You have to believe me."

"I wouldn't trust the likes of you if you paid me," Mr Chadwick said as he aimed another blow.

Charles was trying to stand up, and the punch skimmed off the side of his head almost knocking him over again.

"Father, stop," Mary cried.

"I wouldn't do anything to hurt her." Charles ducked again, and a punch, aimed at his stomach, landed squarely on his shoulder.

"Get out of here and don't let me ever see you again. You damn Quakers have got no morals. Your sister's proof enough of that." Mr Chadwick grabbed a pitchfork from the corner of the barn and charged at him.

Charles saw him coming and threw himself out of the way, but Mr Chadwick turned and came at him again. Fearing he was about to be pinned to the ground, Charles scrambled to his feet and ran from the barn.

"Father, stop, please," Mary begged as she ran after them. "It wasn't like that."

"You get back to the house. I'll deal with you later."

With Mr Chadwick still chasing him, Charles ran through the gate and didn't stop until the farmhouse was out of sight. Sure he was alone, he slowed to a walk but hadn't gone far before he needed to sit down. The grass verge was wet, but he didn't care. His heart was thumping, the punches to his stomach had made him feel sick, and it was as if someone had plunged a knife into his shoulder. Thank God the blow to his head had only grazed him. He would have been out cold had it connected properly. Not that any of those things mattered. He was more concerned about what would happen to Mary. He needed to know she was safe, but he daren't go back. Not tonight at any rate.

It took Charles almost two hours to walk back to Aldridge. As he walked into the kitchen, his father was sitting by the fire drying his feet.

"It's about time," he said. "I was expecting you over a week ago. What kept you?"

"It's that fool Chadwick. Not got a clue what he's doing. Had nowhere near enough men." Charles went to the table and cut himself a slice of bread.

"That's no reason to keep you. The deal was you went for a month, not six weeks."

"Well, I'm here now. What do you want me to do?"

"For a start, you can renew your game certificate. We're being overrun with hares from the woods and I want them dealt with."

*

The smell of bacon floating into the bedroom woke Charles. As soon as he remembered where he was, he tried to jump out of bed but fell back onto the mattress as a pain shot through his shoulder. Damn that fool man. Moving more carefully, he swung his legs out of bed and went to the dresser where he threw some water on his face. He needed to move faster than this. The last thing he wanted was for his father to think he was work-shy. It took him less than two minutes to get dressed, but by the time he arrived for breakfast his father had gone. Breathing a sigh of relief, he stopped to tuck his shirt into his trousers.

"What time do you call this?" his mother said. "Another five minutes and you'd have been going without. Sit yourself down quickly."

"Where is everybody?" Charles asked.

"Pa's gone to Birmingham and everyone else is doing their jobs. In case you haven't noticed, we've got the harvest to get in. Why your father agreed to let you work in Shenstone, I don't know. We haven't got enough hands as it is."

"Well, I'm here now. I'll go and help Richard when I've had something to eat and go to Lichfield for the certificate this afternoon."

"Are you going to tell me what happened in Shenstone?"

"I told you." Charles shifted in his seat.

"No you didn't." His mother put a plate of bacon in front of him and folded her arms, waiting for an explanation. "Mr Chadwick being a fool is no reason to delay you and it doesn't explain that gash on the side of your head."

Charles ran his fingers over the cut on his temple.

"It's nothing, just a cut."

"It looks like more than a cut to me and where's your bag? You came back with nothing last night."

"I left in a hurry." He dumped his bacon between two slices of buttered bread and marched to the door. "I'll see you later."

Charles walked straight across the kitchen window to make sure his mother saw him, but once he rounded the corner of the house, he sat down and took a bite out of his sandwich. He had planned on helping his brother this morning, but he wasn't doing any digging with his shoulder the way it was. He needed to see Mary, too. If he timed it right, he could go to Shenstone on his way to Lichfield and hope that Mr Chadwick was in the fields. Whether he would be able to see Mary was another matter, but he had to try.

The lanes were quiet as he walked and he only saw a couple of women making their way to the village. As he approached the farm, he hesitated. Should he go and knock on the door or wait and hope that Mary came out by herself. Feeling his shoulder, he decided to wait and sat behind a hedge where he could see the farmyard. Mrs Chadwick was in and out of the house regularly, but he didn't see anyone else for over an hour until Mary walked out of the back door. He was about to call her when Alice followed and linked her arm with her sister's to walk over to the barn.

They're not going to let her out on her own, Charles thought. *Not even to the barn. No wonder she looks so miserable.* He waited for them to reappear, hoping to catch her eye, but when he saw the expression on Alice's face, he knew he needed to leave her alone. Alice was there to guard her, not keep her company. He needed to work out how he was going to see her again without getting her into more trouble. He couldn't just march up to the door and hope for the best. Within a minute, Mary was back in the house and Alice scanned the yard before she too disappeared.

Reluctantly, when he realised Mary was unlikely to come out again, he stood up and started his walk to Lichfield. His pace was slow as he considered his options and the whole trip took longer than expected.

It was almost time for tea when he returned home with his game certificate. He passed his mother in the yard and walked into the kitchen to find Louisa feeding her young daughter. He flopped into the chair opposite her.

"Ann's growing up fast." He nodded at his niece. "Two in a couple of weeks, isn't she?"

"She is, but I don't know what I'm going to do with her. I can't hide her away as easily as I used to."

"You don't need to hide her, not around here. Folks know it wasn't your fault."

"They still don't want anything to do with me, though."

"The downside of living in a place like Aldridge, I suppose," Charles said. "Maybe you should go to Birmingham and leave her with Mother. You'd be able to hold your head up again down there."

"Don't think I haven't thought about it. Maybe next year."

"What about next year?" their mother asked as she entered the kitchen.

"Just wondering when I might go to Birmingham again. I haven't been since Ann was born."

"Don't you start. It's bad enough your sister being down there. What's wrong with Aldridge?"

"Nothing." Louisa rolled her eyes at Charles. "Here, let me help you. I've finished with Ann and everyone will be back and wanting their tea before we know it."

Louisa placed the baby on Charles's knee while she set the table. She was a sweet child with her dark curly hair and rosy cheeks, and Charles relaxed into the chair while she played with the buttons on his waistcoat.

"Don't let her go to sleep," Louisa said. "I want her awake for at least another hour before I put her in her cot."

"Charles won't let her go to sleep," her mother said. "He's usually the one who winds her up just before bedtime."

"Not tonight, I won't. I'm tired myself for some reason. The way I feel at the moment, I'll be going to bed at the same time as her."

"What's the matter with you?" his mother asked.

"I've had a headache coming on all afternoon."

"It'll be that cut on your head. I told you it was more than nothing." His mother walked over and inspected the graze again. "How did you do it?"

"I got too close to a broken tree branch," Charles lied. "Now can you give me five minutes peace to see if I can be rid of it?"

He didn't get his five minutes. Moments later, his father and brother walked in and once his younger sisters joined them, he knew there was no chance of a nap. With a sigh of resignation he put Ann on the floor and went to the table.

"Are you all right?" Louisa said as he sat next to her.

"Not really, but don't make a fuss. As soon as I've had something to eat I'm going to sneak off to bed. Hopefully no one will miss me."

*

He woke early the next morning and although his head had cleared, a sense of foreboding hung over him. He had seen Mary in his dreams, as clearly as if she were standing in the room with him, but she hadn't been happy. She'd been pleading with him to go and get her, and although he knew it was only a dream, he couldn't help thinking she really was calling out to him.

He pulled on his trousers and decided he needed a clean shirt. As soon as he'd eaten breakfast, he was going over to Shenstone to get her. He needed to look his best.

"Where do you think you're going?" his mother said as soon as he entered the kitchen.

"What do you mean?"

"You've got your best shirt on. You're not working in that; I'll never get it clean."

"I've got an errand to run. I won't be long."

"You're right you won't be long, because you're not going anywhere," his father cut in. "Those hares are causing untold damage to the carrots and turnips, and I want them dealt with. This morning."

He was about to object but thought better of it. He didn't want to mention what had happened in Shenstone and didn't actually know that Mary was in trouble. He could go later.

Once he changed his shirt he went to the outhouse to get his gun and walked across the fields with Richard.

"I'm glad you're back," his brother said. "Father's had me doing everything round here. Get a move on with the hares will you, then you can come and help me with the carrots."

"I'll be as long as it takes. They don't all come out of hiding and surrender, you know. Besides, I need to slip off."

"You heard what Father said. Not today. We have to get these crops in before the weather turns. There'll be plenty of time for sloping off when we're done."

Charles quickened his pace into the woods before he was tempted to tell Richard what he could do with the crops. If he wanted to go to Shenstone, he would. Once hidden from view, he stood with his hands on his hips, considering his options. The only thing he cared about was Mary. He needed to go to her, but within a minute, several hares ran past him and he knew he daren't leave until he'd dealt with them.

He was busy for the rest of the day until he heard Richard shouting to him.

"Are you finished? It's time to go." Charles didn't need asking twice and was out of the wood in seconds. "Sounds like you've had a good day if all those shots hit their target."

"I got a lot of them, but I'll have to set some traps tomorrow for the rest. I'm sure they think it's a game."

Richard laughed. "You're right, but never mind that, as long as you haven't damaged them too badly we'll be having a nice bit of meat for the next few weeks. What have you done with them?"

"I've hidden them in the woods. I'll pick them up tomorrow when I've finished."

"That'll be a nice job for Mother, hanging them all. It'll take her hours."

As they reached the house, they both washed their hands and Charles put his gun in the outhouse before he went to the kitchen. Richard was still in the doorway, blocking his way. He was about to ask him to move when he saw two police constables standing in front of the hearth.

"Here he is, constable." His mother grabbed his arm and pulled him inside. "What have you been up to, Charles Jackson?"

"Nothing, why?"

"We have reason to believe you've been thieving in Shenstone and need to ask you a few questions," the older of the policemen said.

A nervous smile broke on his face and he looked at his mother.

"I haven't been to Shenstone today."

"Maybe not, but were you in Shenstone on Thursday just gone?"

"He was back here by then," his mother said. "Left Shenstone on Wednesday, he did."

"I need the suspect to answer if you don't mind, Mrs Jackson." The constable turned back to Charles. "Well, laddie, what do you have to say?"

Charles coughed to clear the lump that had formed in his throat. "I went to Lichfield on Thursday to get a game certificate. You can check with them."

"You must have passed through Shenstone on your way there."

"I didn't stop, just kept walking."

"But that places you in Shenstone on Thursday. Take your boots off; we need to measure your left foot."

"What am I supposed to have done?"

"There was a serious theft and you've been reported as being in the area. Now, if you'll let us measure your foot, we'll be on our way."

It was another five minutes before the policemen left and Charles collapsed into the nearest chair.

"What have you been up to?" his mother asked.

"I haven't been up to anything."

"You wouldn't have the police asking after you if you'd done nothing. Just you wait until your father gets in. He'll want to know the truth."

Charles didn't have long to wait before his father arrived, and he closed his eyes while his mother recounted the policemen's visit.

"You've got some explaining to do." His father came and stood over him. "You were supposed to be helping Richard on Thursday morning, but you didn't show up. Why not?"

"I needed to clear my head and so I walked to Lichfield."

"You walked to Lichfield? Are you mad?" His father turned away and paced the kitchen, his face turning crimson. "We've got the harvest to bring in and you're going for a walk. I'm not surprised you were gone so long."

"Leave him alone," Louisa said as she stood up from her seat in the corner. "He wasn't well on Thursday. If you remember he went to bed early and didn't come down again until the next day."

"Maybe it was his guilty conscience," Richard said. "Leaving me to do all the heavy lifting while he was *clearing his head*. Not to mention what he might have been up to in Shenstone."

"Stop it." Charles jumped from his chair. "I haven't done anything wrong and I certainly didn't steal anything from Shenstone. Don't bother serving me anything to eat. I'm going to the tavern."

*

It was Monday evening before the constables returned, and as before, they stood by the hearth waiting for Charles to arrive home. This time there were no pleasantries.

"Charles Jackson, we are arresting you for the reported larceny of a cheese, seven hams, and assorted other items from a house in Shenstone on the night of Thursday, August fifteenth. We're here to take you to the lock-up in Lichfield from where you will be transported to Stafford Gaol to await trial."

Charles clutched the nearest chair as a wave of nausea washed over him.

"I haven't stolen anything. Mother, tell them. I wasn't in Shenstone on Thursday night."

"That's right, Constable, he wasn't."

"I'm sorry, Son, but you'll have to save that for the magistrate. We have a witness who saw you and an accomplice carrying a couple of heavy sacks and acting suspiciously. Your boot size matches the footprint at the scene of the crime too."

"There must be hundreds of men wearing the same boots as me. You can't lock me up for that."

"Constable please," his mother said as she saw him remove a set of handcuffs from his belt. "You can't take him, he's only a minor."

"He's a minor who couldn't keep his hands to himself."

"It wasn't him. He's a good lad. He doesn't deserve to be locked up."

Charles struggled to free himself as his mother argued, but the second constable held him firm until his arms were fastened securely behind his back. His mother tried to pull him free, but the older constable grabbed her arms.

"Come here, Ma." Louisa took her mother in her arms. "We'll get him out. Pa will know what to do."

Charles tried to resist as the constables forced him through the door, but once he was outside, there was nothing he could do.

"Tell Pa to come for me," he shouted as he was dragged into a carriage. "I haven't done anything."

The sun had been high in the sky when he left Aldridge, but by the time he reached Lichfield, it was close to the horizon. Not that it mattered. As soon as he was thrown into one of the cells, it could have been the middle of the night; such was the depth of the darkness. A guard followed him into the cell, attached a night light to the wall, and walked out, slamming the door behind him. As his eyes adjusted to the light, Charles saw a bench against one wall. It was the only thing in the cell, but as he moved towards it, his foot kicked something soft that let out a squeal before it scurried away.

He kicked the underside of the bench before he sat down in case anything was lurking, but when he leaned back on the wall, he immediately jumped forward again. The wall was soaking wet and hummed as he put his head near it. How had he come to be here? It was less than a week ago that he'd held Mary in his arms, and now he wasn't sure when he would even see her again. He pictured her face as he'd held it between his hands, the blue of her eyes vivid in his darkness. With some difficulty, he curled up on the bench and let his tears flow.

At some point he must have fallen asleep, because he was woken with a start by the sound of banging. He had no idea what time it was but several minutes later, the door to his cell opened and he was grabbed by the arms and forced to stand up.

"What's going on?"

"Time for a walk," the guard said. "You get ten minutes of exercise every morning and afternoon. You're lucky today, it's not raining."

"Can't you take these cuffs off me?"

"When you get back. There'll be bread and water waiting for you. I'll sort you out then."

Charles wondered at the need for such security. The exercise yard was no more than ten feet square and was surrounded by walls twice as high. Even without the cuffs, he wouldn't be going anywhere.

The yard was quiet, with only two other inmates, but talking was forbidden. Charles did as he was told and walked around the square at a regular pace. It was too early in the day for the sun to peer over the walls, but he relished the smell of fresh air after the stench of the cell. All too soon, the ten minutes were up and the guard ushered him back inside.

After eating the meagre slice of bread and with his arms now free, he lay back on the bench to consider who could have seen him in Shenstone. As far as he was aware, he hadn't seen anyone he knew, and while he was at Chadwick's farm, he had been alone. What was he missing?

He was disturbed from his thoughts by the guard opening the door. He assumed it was time for his afternoon exercise and stood up, but the guard closed the door and raised some shackles in front of him.

"The others didn't have cuffs on this morning. Why do I need them?"

"I need to take you to the front of the building. You have a visitor. Come and stand by the candle so I can see what I'm doing."

The guard led Charles down the corridor towards the large metal gate barring the entrance. On the other side, he saw his father waiting for him.

"Pa, you've got to get me out of here," he shouted when he saw his father. "I can't stay here another night."

"It's not as simple as that," his father said, the colour draining from his face as he saw his youngest son with chains around his wrists and ankles. "You have to be honest with me. Did you take those hams and cheese?"

"Of course I didn't! You shouldn't even need to ask."

"Someone thinks you did. Have you any idea why?"

"I don't know, Pa. Truly, I don't. If I could get out of here, I'd ask around."

"You're not going anywhere," the guard said as he kept hold of his arm. "You're in for a serious charge, and no magistrate's going to let you out before you've had a trial by jury. The chances are you'll be going to Stafford in the next few days."

"You can't send him there. He's only a minor."

"I'm only telling you what I've heard."

"Please, Pa, isn't there anything you can do?" Charles reached through the bars and grabbed his father's arm.

"I don't know where I'm going to start." Mr Jackson took off his cap and scratched his head. "I need to find a solicitor first. I don't know how much this is going to cost me, but if I spend money only to find out you did steal the stuff, I'll disown you."

"I swear, honest I didn't do it. You have to get me out of here."

*

Three weeks passed before Charles saw his father again. The guard came to collect him and led him to a communal area where he was sitting with a solicitor. The room wasn't much bigger than the cell he occupied, but it had a small window and Charles had to shield his eyes from the light.

"What's happened to you?" Mr Jackson said as Charles sat down. "You look dreadful."

"It's not exactly home from home. The place is filthy. I've nothing but a board to sleep on, and all I get to eat is a piece of bread in the morning and one in the evening. Ask Mother to send me some food next time you come."

"You wouldn't keep animals in conditions like this," Mr Jackson said to the solicitor.

"They treat animals better than they treat us. The lad in the cell next to mine sounds close to death. He's always coughing and crying out in pain. If he were an animal, they'd have shot him long ago."

"Can I bring you back to the discussions for today?" Mr Adams said. "We don't have much time." He opened a file and rifled through it. "Let me tell you what I've learned since you chose to engage my services. As you know, Charles has been charged with stealing one cheese, seven hams, a razor, a chisel and a vermin-trap. The prosecutor says he has a witness who saw him with two sacks and two bags that could have contained the stolen items. They also claim you tried to sell the cheese to Mrs Parsons. Do you have anything to say?"

"Where did they see me?"

Mr Adams looked down at his notes.

"In Squire Lee Woods. The witness said he helped you over the hedge."

Charles tried to remember the afternoon. He was so hungry, it was difficult to remember yesterday, much less weeks ago, but slowly his memory returned.

"I was in the woods that day, but I was shooting hares. Richard'll back me up; he heard me. The bags were full of them. Pa, you know how many hares we had running over the place. I was getting rid of them like you told me to."

"What did you do with them?" Mr Adams asked.

"Parsons came to help me and we hid them in some bushes to save carrying them back. I was going to sell a few, and he did offer one to his wife, but when we went back the next day, they were gone."

"Do you know why anyone would want to conspire against you?" Mr Adams said.

"Why would anyone do that?" Mr Jackson said. "We're a respectable family; we wouldn't harm anyone."

"I need to ask the question," Mr Adams said. "Charles, do you have anything to say?"

Charles sat thinking, then the blood drained from his face.

"It's him," he said, spitting out his words.

"Who? What are you talking about?" his father said.

"It's that fool Chadwick; he's set me up."

"Why would he do that?"

"Because ... because ..." Charles realised he had never explained what happened in Shenstone.

"Did you take something from him?"

Only his daughter's heart, Charles thought. "Not exactly."

"You're going to have to do better than that if you want us to help," his father said. "You'd better tell us what happened."

Charles felt his cheeks burning as he stared at his hands, struggling to find the right words.

"We had an argument," he said. Then he took a deep breath and told them everything.

*

Six weeks later, Mr Adams succeeded in persuading a magistrate to release Charles to await his trial at home. His father took a carriage to pick him up. When they got home and walked through the door, his mother burst into tears.

"What have they done to you?" she sobbed as she wrapped her arms around him. "There's almost nothing left of you, and look at that horrible beard. Come and sit next to me. I've made your favourite tea."

"I don't know that I'll be able to finish it," Charles said. "Other than the food you've sent, I've not eaten much. At least I've been sleeping better since the lad in the cell next to me died. Consumption they said it was. It was quiet with him gone."

"Come on, try and eat something before the others come in." His mother put a plate of beef and kidney pie in front of him, but Charles ignored her.

"Someone in the lock up reckons I could be transported if they find me guilty."

"I don't doubt it," his father said. "Why do you think I hired Mr Adams? Cost me a small fortune, I don't mind saying, but folks around here say he's the best."

"I swear I'll repay you once this is over."

*

The trial was held at the end of December and as he was led into the courtroom he saw his father and mother sitting with Louisa. His mother looked as if she'd been crying, but they smiled when they saw him.

When he was called to the dock, Charles stood with the confidence of someone who knew he had done nothing wrong. Mr Adams had told him there were flaws in the prosecution's argument and it would bode well with the jury if he acted as if he was not guilty.

The trial hadn't long been in progress before Charles realised who had been doing Mr Chadwick's dirty work: Albert Dray, a labourer from Aldridge who had worked with his father for a few days last August. His father had sacked him for missing a day's work and he'd gone to Shenstone while Charles was there. It was clear he knew Mr Chadwick of old, and he'd seen the two of them supping together at the end of the day. If ever there was anyone who would get you into trouble, you could rely on Albert.

His father must have realised the same thing and Charles saw him talking to Mr Adams before he started his cross-examination.

"Mr Dray," the solicitor began, "can you explain to the jury how you know the Jackson family?"

"I done some work on their farm last summer."

"What sort of work?"

"Pulling the potatoes."

"But I believe Mr Jackson senior dismissed you from his employment. Why was that?"

Mr Dray glared at Mr Jackson senior before he answered.

"I din't turn up for work one day. One day, that was all."

"So you don't think you should have lost your job?"

"Would you lose your job if you missed one day?" Mr Dray's voice bellowed around the courtroom. "He had it in for me, he did."

"So you don't think the reason for your absence could have been the reason he dismissed you?"

Mr Dray stared at the solicitor, his lips twitching, but no words coming out.

"I've been led to believe that on the day in question you were being interviewed by the police," Mr Adams continued. "The offence was serious enough that a few weeks after the interview, you went before the magistrates and found yourself in gaol. I would say that Mr Jackson had good reason to dismiss you, wouldn't you?"

"He didn't know they'd find me guilty."

"But guilty you were. Nevertheless, a few days later, you were released. Can you tell the jury how this came about?"

The witness shifted uncomfortably and looked across to the men of the jury.

"They let me go."

"It wasn't quite like that was it, Mr Dray? I put it to you that when you were in gaol, you were given the chance to walk free by promising to testify against young Mr Jackson here. Am I right?"

Mr Dray again said nothing.

"Failing to answer the questions is not going to help your cause, Mr Dray."

"I saw him in the wood looking suspicious … and he had two big bags with him."

"The wood in question is adjacent to his father's fields." Mr Adams turned to the jury. "As for the contents of the bags, he had been shooting hares all afternoon, something he is permitted to do by virtue of the fact he has a game certificate. I put it to you, Mr Dray, that you didn't actually see Mr Jackson with the goods in question. Am I right?"

Mr Dray glanced again at the jury before he nodded his head.

"Thank you. In that case, I have no further questions."

The prosecution called another three witnesses, but all had similar stories. Once the last of them stepped down, Mr Adams took the floor.

"Members of the jury, you see before you a young man who has been charged with larceny in the absence of any evidence. You have not heard one witness this afternoon able to confirm they saw Mr Jackson with the hams and cheese, and yet the potential sentence for a crime of this nature would be significant. I suggest to you that the case for the prosecution was nothing more than a foul conspiracy against my client. If any more evidence is needed to prove the point, I would like to call Miss Louisa Jackson, sister of the defendant."

Louisa took the stand and after swearing her oath, stood up straight and faced Mr Adams.

"Miss Jackson, can you explain to the jury how you know that your brother is innocent?"

Charles knew what she was going to say but still marvelled at the way she handled herself under the circumstances. She confirmed that Charles couldn't have taken the items. He had been into Lichfield that day to renew his game certificate and had come home and eaten tea, but shortly afterwards had gone to bed with a headache.

At least that punch from Mr Chadwick was of some use, Charles thought as he rubbed the side of his head.

Mr Adams thanked her, and as she walked back to her seat, Charles winked at her, forcing a weak smile onto her previously stern face.

Although Charles had appeared confident all afternoon, once the Not Guilty verdict was returned, his calm demeanour disappeared and he shook from head to toe. Several men had been sentenced to years of transportation for far lesser crimes that day, and the enormity of what could have been washed over him.

"Come on, let's get you home." His mother linked his arm to escort him from the courthouse.

"I need to get away from here," he said once they were in the carriage. "There are folks around here who have it in for me."

"Now you know how I feel," Louisa said.

"Come with me. The three of us can go to Birmingham and get away from all this."

"Three?" Louisa and his mother spoke in unison.

For the first time in his life, Charles blushed.

"What haven't you told us?" His mother was clearly annoyed.

"He's found himself a woman, or should I say girl," Mr Jackson answered. "Although she's not just any girl."

"Who is she?" Louisa was used to being Charles's confidant and was stung by the fact that he hadn't told her first.

"I'm sorry. I wanted to tell you, but once I was in the lock up, I didn't have a chance. Her name's Mary and she lives in Shenstone."

"Her name's Mary Chadwick," Mr Jackson said. "And her father's the bounder who tried to get Charles transported to Australia."

Charles wished he could disappear when his mother glared at him.

"What have you been doing? You haven't got her in the family way, have you?"

"Of course I haven't. After what happened to Louisa, I wouldn't do that to anyone."

"Is that why you had the cut on your head? If it is, you're not going back. There's no telling what her father will do. I knew you weren't telling me the truth."

"I don't care what he'll do. I'll be ready for him this time. I promised Mary I'd go back and I'm not going to abandon her. Besides, before I left Shenstone, I asked her to marry me, and she said yes."

His mother sat with her mouth open as the implications of what he'd said hit her.

"You've known for almost five months that you were getting married and you didn't tell anyone?" Louisa said. "How old is she?"

"Same age as me; nineteen."

"Well, her father's not going to give his consent, is he?"

"He will," Charles said. "Getting witnesses to give false testimony is a criminal offence. He won't want anyone to know he was behind it."

"You can't prove it."

"If someone's guilty, the mere suggestion that they might be investigated will be enough. Chadwick won't want his reputation ruined."

*

Mr Jackson insisted on accompanying Charles to Shenstone in case there was any trouble. It was a bitter evening and Mr Chadwick beckoned them in as much to close the door as to be hospitable. When Charles saw Mary sitting by the fire with her mother and sisters he knew he'd been right to come back. Her eyes came to life and a smile spread across her face.

"What are you doing here?" her father asked once the door was shut. "I told you I didn't want to see you again."

"There was no need to try and get him transported, though, was there?" Mr Jackson said.

Charles watched his father with admiration. Why couldn't he be so assertive?

"I don't know what you mean." Mr Chadwick took a step backwards.

"I think you do." His father stepped forward and Charles heard a gasp from beside the fire. He turned to see the concern on Mary's face as his father took another step forward, his eyes focussing on no one but Mr Chadwick. "Arthur Dray wasn't quite the witness you hoped for, was he?"

"I hardly know the man."

"You seem to be making a habit of lying." Mr Jackson took hold of the front of Mr Chadwick's shirt. "It's about time people around here knew the truth about you."

"What do you want?" Mr Chadwick said, the pitch of his voice betraying his fear.

With another glance at Mary, Charles took hold of his father's shoulders and manoeuvred him away from Mr Chadwick. He then stepped forward and addressed Mr Chadwick himself.

"I've come for Mary," he said, his voice level and calm. "I'm moving to Birmingham, and I want her to join me as my wife."

Mary dropped her mending and ran to Charles, throwing her arms around his neck.

"I thought they were going to send you away," she said, tears streaming down her cheeks.

"Go and sit down this minute." Mr Chadwick pushed her to one side.

"She'll do no such thing." Charles put himself between Mary and her father.

"Is it true it was you who tried to get him sent away?" Mary said over Charles's shoulder.

"He's no good for you. If you go with him, don't ever think about coming back," Mr Chadwick said. "I'll be finished with you."

"No," her mother cried as she joined the group. "You can't let her go."

"If she thinks she can marry a Quaker and still be part of this family, she can think again."

"She won't be coming back," Charles said. "We're going to Birmingham and I'm going to get a job in a brass foundry."

"Stop!" Mrs Chadwick shouted to make herself heard before turning to Mary. "What do you want? Tell me you don't want to go."

Mary couldn't stop her tears and clung to Charles for support.

"I love him," she said through her sobs. "I want to be with him. Please let me go."

A look of pain crossed Mrs Chadwick's face and she turned to Charles, her hatred evident.

"We treated you like one of the family and this is how you repay us. My daughter was perfectly happy until you turned up. She won't last five minutes down there and you'll destroy her reputation."

"We're getting married."

It was Mrs Chadwick now who walked towards Charles, poking him in the chest.

"And who d'you think will preside over the service? No one in the Church of England will marry a Quaker, and the services your lot have aren't legal."

"Of course they're legal, but if it matters that much, we'll get married in one of *your* churches. They're a bit more tolerant in Birmingham."

"If you love her, you won't tear her from her family."

"If you love her, you won't throw her out."

"Stop, please." Mary threw her arms around her mother. "Don't be angry. Can't you be happy for me?"

"Get off me." Mrs Chadwick pushed Mary from her. "If you want to go with him, go and pack your bags now because you're not staying here."

Mary fell back onto Charles, her eyes wide in disbelief. She looked at her father and then to her sisters, who sat open mouthed at the other side of the room. Charles held her tightly, savouring having her in his arms until she pulled herself up to her full height and headed for the stairs.

The room was silent as everyone watched her go, before Alice moved to comfort her mother and Mr Chadwick reached for the door.

"Get out of my house. Now. And when I say I don't ever want to see you again, I mean it."

"I'm not going without Mary."

"You'll wait outside for her." Mr Chadwick pushed Charles through the door, causing him to land in a heap on the floor. "May the Lord avenge you for this."

"She'd better be worth it," his father said as the door slammed behind them.

It was another fifteen minutes before the door opened again. Charles stepped forward but Mary came out with such force that she ended up on the ground in much the same way he had. He ran to help her and only narrowly missed being hit by the bag thrown out seconds later.

"Don't ever bother coming back," her father shouted as he slammed the door.

Mary was inconsolable on the journey back to Aldridge and Charles hated himself for causing her so much pain. He asked if she wanted to go back and forget about him, but that had brought more tears and she clung to him as if her life depended on him.

Once they got home, his mother took her upstairs and left him sitting by the fire with his father and a glass of ale. An hour later Mary came back down, her tear stained face scrubbed and her hair brushed neatly down her back. He stood up, not knowing what to say, but when she smiled, he knew he'd done the right thing.

That night, the strains of the previous five months were forgotten and he fell asleep dreaming of his bride. Her smile, her beautiful blue eyes, her touch. He remembered her as she kissed his hands, his neck, his cheeks, his lips. She was going to make him the happiest man alive.

He was brought back from his memories by the sound of crying. His daughter must have been asleep in her pram beneath the window, but Mary's voice, calm and soothing, quietened her as she brought her inside. He smiled momentarily when he thought of the joy his son and daughter had brought him, but it faded when he realised that feeding Mary Ann would keep Mary downstairs for a little longer. How he wished she would come up and see him. Charles rolled his head to the side to see Louisa. She deserved a better life than this. If only she'd stayed in Birmingham with him and Mary, she might have found a husband by now, but she'd missed her daughter too much and returned home to be with her. He couldn't blame her. He'd made the journey himself when the consumption had taken hold of him.

She was sewing now and seemed so absorbed in her work that he didn't want to disturb her. Perhaps it was for the best; it would mean Mary could remain content for a little while longer. He loved her more than life itself and prayed that one day she would be happy again. There would be someone else to take his place, of that he had little doubt. He focussed once more on keeping his breathing stable, but it was shallow and his vision was starting to blacken. After a moment, he stopped fighting and let his eyes close before he offered up one last prayer and let the will of God take him.

Thank you for reading *Condemned by Fate*. I hope you enjoyed it.

If so, please share your thoughts and leave a review here:

myBook.to/CondemnedByFate

It will be greatly appreciated.

I'd love to keep in touch with you!

I send out regular monthly newsletters with details of new releases and special offers.

To keep in touch, visit: **vlmcbeath.com**

After Charles's death, Mary stayed with his family in Aldridge until circumstances forced her to move to Birmingham.

The *Ambition & Destiny* Series tells the story of her survival and of her family's turbulent relationship with the ambitious Mr Wetherby.

For further details visit:

http://Author.to/VLMcBeath

Books in The *Ambition & Destiny* Series

Part 1: *Hooks and Eyes*

To start again, Mary must leave the past behind...

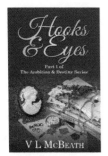

Mary is desperate to put her troubled past behind her. As a widow with two small children, she is determined to earn enough money to look after her family. When she takes a job making hooks & eyes for the ambitious Mr. Wetherby, she thinks she's found a solution...

But when Mr. Wetherby decides he wants Mary as more than a worker, she fears his intentions are dishonorable. After all, why else would he be interested in her? Following a misunderstanding, Mary abandons her job, never wanting to see him again.

While Mary prepares to make another life for herself, Mr. Wetherby has other ideas. If his plan works, he could use the children to win Mary's heart and free her from a life of poverty once and for all...

Inspired by a true story, *Hooks & Eyes* begins an epic saga of one family's trials, tragedies, and triumphs as they seek their fortune in Victorian-era England.

If you like 19th-century historical fiction you'll love the first instalment in this engaging series.

GOLD Quality Mark

"Well constructed with strong characters and an interesting storyline and is deserving of a gold standard." *BooksGoSocial*

To read *Hooks & Eyes* visit:
http://myBook.to/Hooks

Part 2: *Less Than Equals*

As Harriet fights for independence, she refuses to conform to the role expected of her...

Harriet is desperate to be free from her domineering aunt and uncle. But as an unmarried woman with few options, she has no choice but to live under their roof. When a charming man comes to work for them, she thinks she's found her way out...

William has given up his former life to be with Harriet. But despite their marriage and the arrival of two children, he refuses to move to a home of their own. When an argument about their future spirals out of control, the consequences for Harriet are severe...

Banished from her home and family, Harriet refuses to play by the rules. Biding her time she is determined to get her own way. And if her idea works, she could free her family from her uncle's control once and for all...

Less Than Equals is the second book in The *Ambition & Destiny* Series, a Victorian-era historical fiction family saga. If you like heroines who are ahead of their time, then you'll love the second instalment in this engaging series.

GOLD Quality Mark

"This is an excellent book, well written and with impeccable timing. The ending is sure to make readers eager for the next book in the series." *BooksGoSocial*

To read *Less Than Equals* visit:
http://myBook.to/LTEAMZ

Part 3: *When Time Runs Out*

As tensions within the family grow, Harriet's refusal to be silenced could be the undoing of them all...

Harriet won't stand by while her family's inheritance slips through their fingers. Her uncle worked hard to build a stable business before he passed it to her husband William. But when her stepfather-in-law, Mr. Wetherby, presumes ownership of the company, Harriet fights to stand her ground...

William longs for a quiet life, but with a growing family and Harriet's determination to succeed, he stretches himself beyond his means. When Mr. Wetherby refuses to help, only the intervention of William's mother Mary keeps their dream of a better future in reach...

After a tragic twist of fate, collaborating with Mr. Wetherby becomes impossible, and Harriet and William must somehow carve out a living without him. But as tensions in the family business escalate, Harriet may have far more to worry about than pursuing her own ambitions...

When Time Runs Out is the third book in The *Ambition & Destiny* Series. If you like family sagas and accurate historical depictions, you'll love the third book in this captivating series.

GOLD Quality Mark
"This is a beautifully written and edited book ... a continuation of a series that has been a delight throughout." *BooksGoSocial*

To read *When Time Runs Out* visit:
http://myBook.to/WTRO

Part 4: *Only One Winner*

A prosperous father. A headstrong son.
One woman caught in the middle.

Angry and seeking answers, William-Wetherby finds comfort and the promise of love with the family's charming young housekeeper, Lydia. With ideas of his own, however, his father is determined to tear them apart. Enraged that Lydia can never be his, William-Wetherby abandons his home determined to forge his own future.

With his son gone, William throws himself into his work. But when his new business partner's dark secret threatens to dismantle his business, William realizes he can't survive alone. With bankruptcy looming, father and son must find it in their hearts to forgive … before they face a once trusted confidant set on their destruction.

Only One Winner is the fourth book in The *Ambition & Destiny* Series. If you like generation-spanning epics, divided family dynamics, and accurate depictions of life in the 19th century, then you'll love the fourth instalment of this riveting series.

GOLD Quality Mark
"Once again the author has produced an excellent book."
BooksGoSocial

To read *Only One Winner* visit:
http://myBook.to/OnlyOneWinner

Part 5: *Different World*

As William-Wetherby seeks a new life, revenge is the only thing on his mind…

Blackmailed into leaving his hometown, William-Wetherby sets off in search of his brother, Charles. In the five years since they've been together their world has changed and with no one to turn to, he needs a friend. With revenge utmost in their minds, Charles persuades his brother to become a police officer…

Struggling to make ends meet, Bella lives with her mother and the two children they are paid to care for. When a striking young man calls about the room they rent out, their curiosity is piqued. What is he hiding? And why won't he tell them anything about his past?

As his former life is gradually revealed, William-Wetherby looks forward to spending time with Bella. But with secrets of her own, he is forced to confront his own prejudices. Can Bella use her charms to claim her man … or will a final surprise from Mr Wetherby threaten their future happiness?

Different World is the final book in The *Ambition & Destiny* Series. If you are keen to know the fates of the Jacksons and Wetherbys, then you'll love the final instalment of this riveting series.

Publication date July 2018

To read *Different World* visit:
http://Author.to/VLMcBeath

About the Author

Val started researching her family tree back in 2008. At that time, she had no idea what she would find or where it would lead. By 2010, she had discovered a story so compelling, she was inspired to turn it into a novel. Initially writing for herself, the story grew beyond anything she ever imagined and now the first books in The *Ambition & Destiny* Series are a reality.

Prior to writing, Val trained as a scientist and has worked in the pharmaceutical industry for many years. In 2012, she set up her own consultancy business, and currently splits her time between business and writing.

Born and raised in Liverpool (UK), Val now lives in Cheshire with her husband, two daughters and a cat. In addition to family history, her interests include rock music and Liverpool Football Club.

For further information about The *Ambition & Destiny* Series, Victorian History or Val's experiences as she wrote the book, visit her website at: www.vlmcbeath.com

Follow me at:

Website: https://valmcbeath.com

Twitter: https://twitter.com/valmcbeath

Facebook: https://www.facebook.com/VLMcBeath

Pinterest: https://uk.pinterest.com/valmcbeath

Amazon: https://www.amazon.com/VL-McBeath/e/B01N2TJWEX/

BookBub: https://www.bookbub.com/authors/vl-mcbeath

Goodreads:
https://www.goodreads.com/author/show/16104358.V_L_McBeath

Made in the USA
Middletown, DE
20 June 2022